Discos or Dumplings

PRAISE FOR *STORYSHARES*

"One of the brightest innovators and game-changers in the education industry."
– Forbes

"Your success in applying research-validated practices to promote literacy serves as a valuable model for other organizations seeking to create evidence-based literacy programs."
- Library of Congress

"We need powerful social and educational innovation, and Storyshares is breaking new ground. The organization addresses critical problems facing our students and teachers. I am excited about the strategies it brings to the collective work of making sure every student has an equal chance in life."
– Teach For America

"Around the world, this is one of the up-and-coming trailblazers changing the landscape of literacy and education."
- International Literacy Association

"It's the perfect idea. There's really nothing like this. I mean wow, this will be a wonderful experience for young people."   - Andrea Davis Pinkney, Executive Director, Scholastic

"Reading for meaning opens opportunities for a lifetime of learning. Providing emerging readers with engaging texts that are designed to offer both challenges and support for each individual will improve their lives for years to come. Storyshares is a wonderful start."
- David Rose, Co-founder of CAST & UDL

Discos or Dumplings

Emily Sun

STORYSHARES

Story Share, Inc.
New York. Boston. Philadelphia

Storyshares
Story Share, Inc.
24 N. Bryn Mawr Avenue #340
Bryn Mawr, PA 19010-3304
www.storyshares.org

Inspiring reading with a new kind of book.

Interest Level: Middle School
Grade Level Equivalent: 4.2

9798885977197

Book design by Storyshares

Printed in the United States of America

Storyshares Presents

1

"Oh, for Heaven's sake, Emma, what in the world are you eating!"

The shout comes from Aunty, speaking in Chinese and currently standing at the doorway. Her arms are crossed. Creases fold on her forehead like the sand dunes of Colorado. Her jet-black hair is chopped off at shoulder length, swaying from side to side as she shakes her head in disapproval.

Her fingers are long and slender, shaped by hours of practicing piano in her childhood. They dance through the air while she gestures to my bowl of milk with cereal.

She moved here two weeks before Chinese New Year to help us take care of my little sister, Annika, while we prepare for the upcoming party.

She has been picking at every little mistake I make for a week. First, I didn't practice the flute for a full hour every day. Then I forgot to put away the homework papers that I left on the dining table. She even had a problem with me not tying up my hair neatly when going outside. What have I done this time?

"Is that even food?" she keeps screeching. "What kind of middle-class young lady puts bread crumbs in milk and calls it a breakfast?"

I groan, carefully piecing together the little Chinese I know to please my aunt. "It's called cereal, Aunty. Anyway, I need to get to school. My alarm ran out of battery and didn't wake me up," I say as I put the bowl into the dishwasher and push in my chair.

"Do not walk away from me, young lady. Look at your sister," Aunty says, gesturing to Annika. She's sitting quietly in her chair, munching on her porridge stuffed with vegetables and meat leftover from yesterday. "Look what she is eating. That is an example of high-quality Chinese food. You should know better at this age."

Annika stares at me with wide brown eyes full of innocence.

I grit my teeth, trying to bite back harsh words. Here Aunty is, comparing me to a seven-year-old who starts school two hours after me while I am in a rush. Why can't she understand me?

Just as I'm about to turn my head and leave, my mom comes and calmly steps in.

"Now, now, what is all this yelling?" she asks. "Sister, I'm sure Emma was just trying to get to school on time. After all, look at her grades: all As! You should be proud of her for giving our family such a good reputation in terms of education. Also, she will plan the Chinese New Year party this Sunday! She is going to make us proud, sister."

My mom winks and smiles, revealing her dimples. Her silky, black hair is tied in a ponytail and streaked with hints of white fighting to come out at the roots. Tiny brown spots dot her sagging cheeks, but her eyes are still filled with the spark she had years ago when I was Annika's age.

Aunty sighs, "Fine. I will leave this for now. But after this, I don't want to see that filthy breakfast on this table. Now, go off to school."

2

The doorbell rings, a sign of Sunny picking me up to walk to school together. I'm grateful for her excellent timing. I open the door and suck in my breath.

Sunny stands in front of me. She's wearing a plaid skirt that only covers half her thigh and a cropped pink sweater with the words "I'm cute, and I know it" printed in bold, smack in the center.

I'm used to this choice of clothing, but as I look back toward Aunty and her open mouth, I know I am in for a scolding from her.

Aunty mutters under her breath in Chinese so Sunny can't understand. "Oh, my! This is your friend? She dresses so inappropriately! Does she not know it is January?"

Sunny boldly exclaims in her bright personality, "Hey, Em! I'm here to make my daily pickup of the one and only you!" She smiles, revealing all her teeth lined with hot pink metal braces. She greets my family with, "Good morning, you all, and have a wonderful day! Vamos, Emma!"

I force an awkward smile and wave goodbye to the stunned woman standing behind me. "Bye, Aunty. Bye, Mom. Bye, Annika. Have a good day, everyone."

When I step out the door, and Aunty thinks I can't hear her, she mutters, "She doesn't even speak her own language in front of her American friends anymore."

Outside the house, I let out a sigh of relief. "Oh, gosh, I can't stand my aunt."

Sunny pats my back. "Hey, I get you. But anyway, how's that party planning you told me about yesterday?"

I immediately perk up and explain all my plans to my best friend. "So, I was thinking I could add some flashy lights since we're doing it outside at night in the park. We could hang them all over the trees and bushes! It'll look so amazing. My cousins are also coming, so I need to impress them!"

"Great idea! For food, chips, Coke, and ice cream are your go-tos. Trust me. I have so many teenage cousins," Sunny says.

This sounds like a fantastic idea to me at first, but then I remember Aunty's comment about the language change in front of my friends. I'm not sure about my Chinese culture, but I also don't want to disappoint my family. Would all that American food really be the go-to? The thought stays on my mind throughout the school day.

BEEEEP! The bell rings, and we quickly dash to class at the last second.

Discos or Dumplings

3

After school, I settle into the couch with my pencil and notebook, writing up plans for the party. Just then, my mom walks in and plops next to me.

"So, how was school?"

That was her usual question. As always, I answered with, "Decent. We had a math test today. I don't know my score yet."

"Well, my daughter always gets a hundred!" she says. "Are you ready for your Chinese New Year party? I heard Cousin Anjie is coming. I'm looking forward to all the traditional decorations you're going to put up. You have so many to choose! Lanterns, red paper cutouts, and don't forget the tiger symbols for luck in the next lunar year. What have you got so far?"

I immediately feel a gnawing feeling in my stomach. I haven't planned any Chinese things at the party. I know it's Chinese New Year, but I'm not that excited about my culture. I also don't want to disappoint Aunty with my little knowledge of it while trying to plan a party around Chinese culture.

"Umm, I'm not sure. Still planning it!" I grimace and force a smile.

My mom winks and leaves my room. I let out a deep sigh of relief and pick up my notebook to continue brainstorming for my party. I start trying to include something about my culture.

* * *

The next day, I am eating my "authentic Chinese breakfast" when I hear a shrill shriek from my upstairs room.

"Emma! Are these your plans for the party?" The words come from Aunty.

I look up to see her waving my notebook and rushing downstairs. The page detailing my plans flies in the air like a beacon.

"Yes, Aunty, is there something wrong?" I ask.

Her jaw drops. "Indeed there is! Where is the Chinese art, the traditional food, the firecrackers?"

"Well, Aunty, I thought we could do something different this year. Maybe something more... American?" I blink twice, awaiting Aunty's disapproval.

As expected, she shakes her head hard. "Absolutely not. I won't allow this. Start over!"

I am completely done with Aunty, so I burst out without thinking, "I wish I weren't Chinese. Why do you have so many expectations for what I do!" I stomp out of the kitchen and all the way to my room, feeling like smoke should be coming out of my ears.

While I am in my room, the phone rings. I pick it up and am greeted by a bright and loud voice.

"Hey, best friend! It's Sunny. Just wanted to ask if you wanna go shopping with me to get the stuff for your party. We could get Boba after..." She rattles on about the things we could do.

I interrupt her to say, "I just had a pretty intense argument with my aunt. You know how she is. She won't let me do anything I want. I might pass on this and try to make amends." I sigh, just thinking about Aunty.

"Oh, I understand. I have an uncle like that, too. Super strict! It's all good, though. My offer is still out there if you change your mind! Catch ya later." Sunny hangs up and leaves me sitting on my bed, thinking it over.

Suddenly, Mom knocks on my door and cracks it open. "Hey, kiddo. What happened with your aunt down there? Never mind, don't answer that. You two need to figure that out by yourselves soon. Anyway, I came by to tell you that we're planning to make dumplings tomorrow! Wanna help?"

"Umm..." I hesitate before answering. "I might have a little thing planned with Sunny, but I'll see!"

"Oh, no worries, dear." She smiles and closes the door, but before she turns away, I see a hint of sadness pull down the corners of her lips.

I quickly blurt out, "Actually, sure. Why not? It'll be fun."

Mom's eyes immediately light up again, and she nods and turns away.

I plop back onto my bed and stare at the blank, white ceiling. After thinking about it for a few moments, I decide I do need to try to mend my relationship with Aunty. I'll start trying tomorrow.

4

After I brush my hair and eat breakfast on Saturday morning, we prepare the supplies to make dumplings. Well, not "we," more like my parents and Aunty. I know nothing about dumplings, so I just stand in the corner like a statue, not wanting to get in their way. When it's finally time to start, I fumble with the ingredients.

"Mix it like this, Emma." Mom patiently demonstrates, spinning her wooden spoon through the bowl of flour. "It's to make the clumps break up."

I blink, clearly confused, and struggle to move my hand in the same way my mother did. The blocks of flour stubbornly stay in shape.

Still, I decide to keep trying. I watch Mom, who is currently adding in the wet ingredients. I do the same, but I accidentally spill too much water into my batter.

I groan in frustration.

Mom pats my back reassuringly. She starts cruising her rolling pin down the shapeless blob of dough, forming it into a smooth circle.

I try to copy, but my rolling pin staggers through the uneven bumps. I sigh in exasperation.

I look at Annika, who is playfully mushing up leftover dough together. She looks back and chuckles at my disastrous creation. Dad also snickers a little while rolling separate balls of dough into spheres. Out of the corner of my eye, I catch Aunty rolling her eyes and tsking her tongue.

A sudden wave of distress washes over me as I stare at my dough. I feel tears starting to well up in my eyes. I slam down the rolling pin and dash up the stairs, feeling everyone's eyes on me in confusion.

In my room, I start ripping out pages in my notebook and crumpling them up into balls. I think to myself, *If I can't make dumplings, how am I supposed to include Chinese culture in the party?*

Right then, Mom enters the room with worried brown eyes to comfort me. "Wanna talk about it?" she asks.

I huff and melt into my bed. "Nothing has been going right since I decided to plan an Americanized party," I complain. "I really don't feel comfortable expressing my family's culture. Every time I try to act Chinese, I do something wrong."

"I understand you have been feeling pressure from Aunty and the party." She sits down on a desk chair. "I just want you to know, whatever you choose, I'll always be proud of you."

"I know. I just need to figure out what I'm going to do for the party. It's tomorrow!" I groan and pick up my notebook.

My mom smiles. "Why don't you come back to finish up the dumplings, and then we'll talk about it."

I pout my lips but decide to trust my mom. I follow her into the kitchen again. While I was gone, Dad already made ten dumplings. They look dainty and fragile but very delicious.

Annika waves to me. "Sister! Look at my dumpling!" She holds out her splotch of dough and smiles from ear to ear.

I giggle at my little sister's innocence and pick up my rolling pin. As I try to run the cylinder over the clump of dough in front of me, I feel Aunty coming up behind me.

I prepare myself for a scolding. Instead, I feel her soft hands on top of mine, guiding me through the process. I turn my head to see her eyes soften and curve into crescent shapes.

Suddenly, it isn't embarrassing to make dumplings, and a realization sparks in my brain. After we plop the different-shaped dumplings into the boiling water to cook, I go up to my room and start replanning my Chinese-American party. I also call Sunny to discuss my plans, and she is all in.

5

On the day of the party, I set up the food — fried dumplings, potato chips, and Chinese sweet herbal tea — and greet all the guests.

The disco ball shines over the dance floor, and red lanterns line the sides of the room.

My cousins come up to me. "Hey, Emma! I haven't seen you in a long time. This party is amazing!" says Xiao Mei, while moving her hips to the music booming in the background.

"The food is great, especially the dumplings," adds Xiao Pang, biting into the juicy meat.

Bouncing excitedly, the youngest of the three, Xiao Li, says, "And the disco ball is such a fun add-on."

"Great job," they all say together. They laugh and walk away, arm in arm, to the dance floor.

I feel pride surge up inside me. Standing by the wall, Aunty smiles at me and waves. She is holding a bag of potato chips, munching happily on them.

Chinese and American dialects crowd my ears, but I can only think about how I embraced my Chinese-American culture. I could never hide being Chinese, but now I have learned to express it proudly in my own way.

About The Author

Emily Sun is a cheerful and bright bookworm who lives on the sunny shores of California. She gets her inspiration from the numerous novels she reads and adores.

If you don't find Emily scribbling ideas for stories in her bedroom, you can find her walking on the beach enjoying the ephemeral waves.

About The Publisher

Story Shares is a nonprofit focused on supporting the millions of teens and adults who struggle with reading by creating a new shelf in the library specifically for them. The ever-growing collection features content that is compelling and culturally relevant for teens and adults, yet still readable at a range of lower reading levels.

Story Shares generates content by engaging deeply with writers, bringing together a community to create this new kind of book. With more intriguing and approachable stories to choose from, the teens and adults who have fallen behind are improving their skills and beginning to discover the joy of reading. For more information, visit storyshares.org.

Easy to Read. Hard to Put Down.